Alexander's Journey with Jesus

Alexander's Journey with Jesus

By Ashton Bohannon

Illustrated by Jason Velazquez

Xulon Press
2301 Lucien Way #415
Maitland, FL 32751
407.339.4217
www.xulonpress.com

Unless otherwise indicated, Scripture quotations taken from the New King James Version (NKJV). Copyright © 1982 by Thomas Nelson, Inc. Used by permission. All rights reserved.

Printed in the United States of America.

Paperback ISBN-13: 978-1-66283-142-3
Hardcover ISBN-13: 978-1-66283-143-0
Ebook ISBN-13: 978-1-66283-144-7

This book is dedicated to my son, Alexander Bohannon.

Alexander was an active participant, as well as a valuable contributor in the creation of this book. He helped me to bring the character to life within the story. We used many real life examples so that the character's traits, interests, and personality resemble the real Alexander! Even many of the phrases we used in the book are things that we say in our house on a regular basis. Alexander loves cars, construction sites, construction vehicles, and Jesus. We wanted to share the love of these things with others in a way that would inspire them to make good decisions and become the best version of themselves.

I admire my son's adoration for life, his passion for the things he loves, and his commitment to his convictions. He has been made in the image of God, and he is valuable, unique, and special. I hope publishing this book will solidify in his heart and soul that he has been made with a purpose, and that he has already made an impact in the world for good, at three years old. It's never too early to start helping others and bringing new people into the kingdom of God.

It was a cool and sunny morning when Alexander decided
he was going to go for a ride in his Volkswagen Beetle.
He couldn't help but notice that something felt different.
He knew he must have forgotten something, but what?

Alexander started his car's engine, and with a mighty roar, the car was ready to go. Alexander's favorite thing to do was drive his car. He loved cars, and he always had, for as long as he could remember. He shifted the car into drive and off he went down his long, gravel driveway.

"That's it!" he exclaimed. "I forgot to pick up my friend."

In the past, Alexander got lost when he tried to find the right way to go without his friend's help.

"My friend is probably waiting on me and wondering where I am," he said. Sure enough, before Alexander could get to the end of his driveway, he saw his friend waiting to be picked up.

Alexander pulled the car up beside his friend and unlocked the car door. Jesus climbed into the passenger's seat of the car.

"Hi Alexander! It's good to see you," Jesus said,

with excitement in His voice.

"It's good to see you too, Jesus. You are a very important

part of my car ride adventure," Alexander said.

"As the GPS of the car, you will tell me where I am and where I need to be going. You will also redirect me when I take a wrong turn or get off track from the path we need to be on, right?" Alexander asked.

"That's right Alexander! As long as you want My help, I will help guide you on this journey," Jesus said.

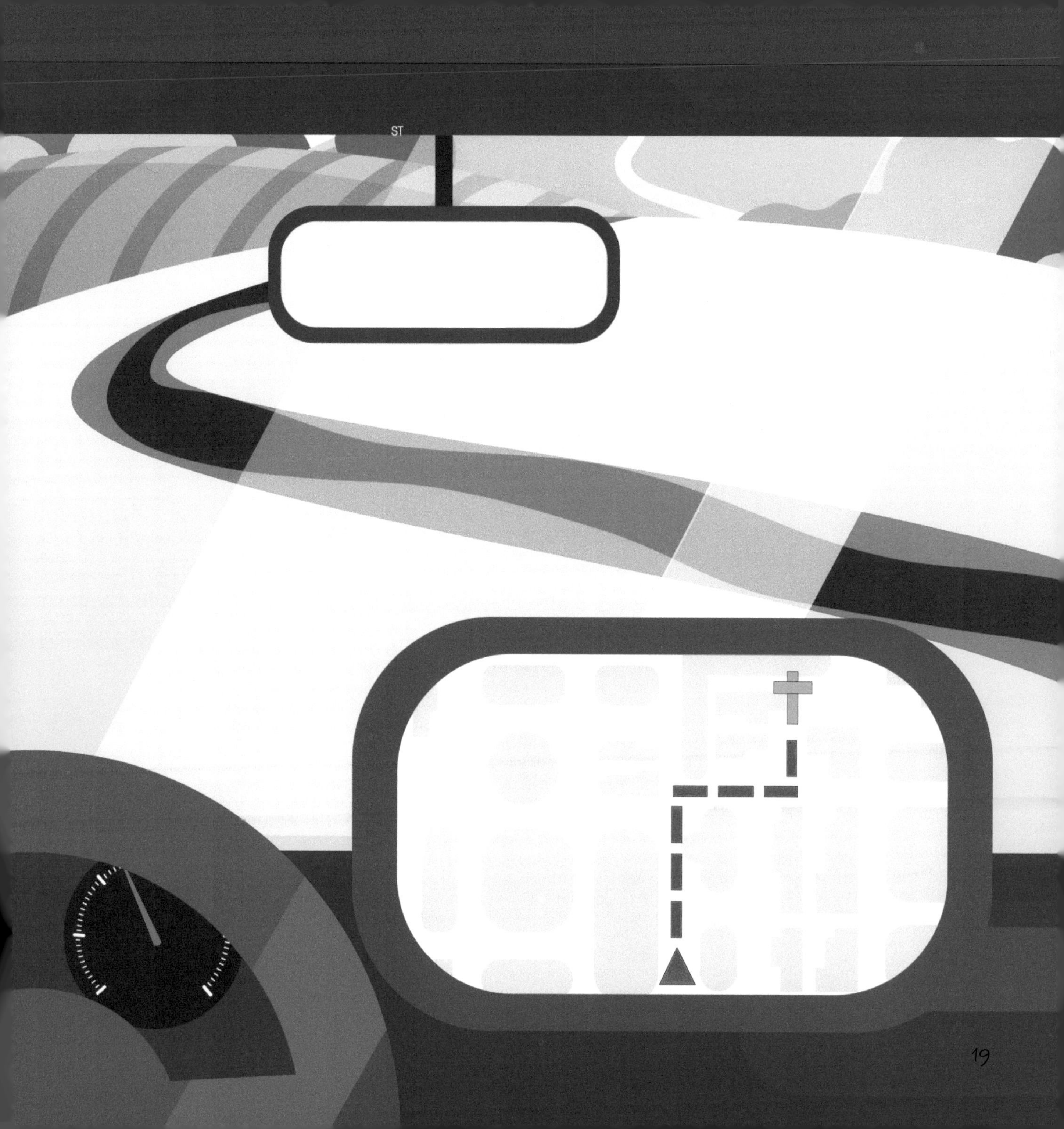

"Awesome! Then we are ready to roll! 1, 2, 3! Let's go! Vrooooom! Vroooom!" Alexander hit the gas pedal, and the car accelerated down the curvy back roads where he lived. Alexander had driven these roads a million times before, and he was sure he knew what to expect up ahead.

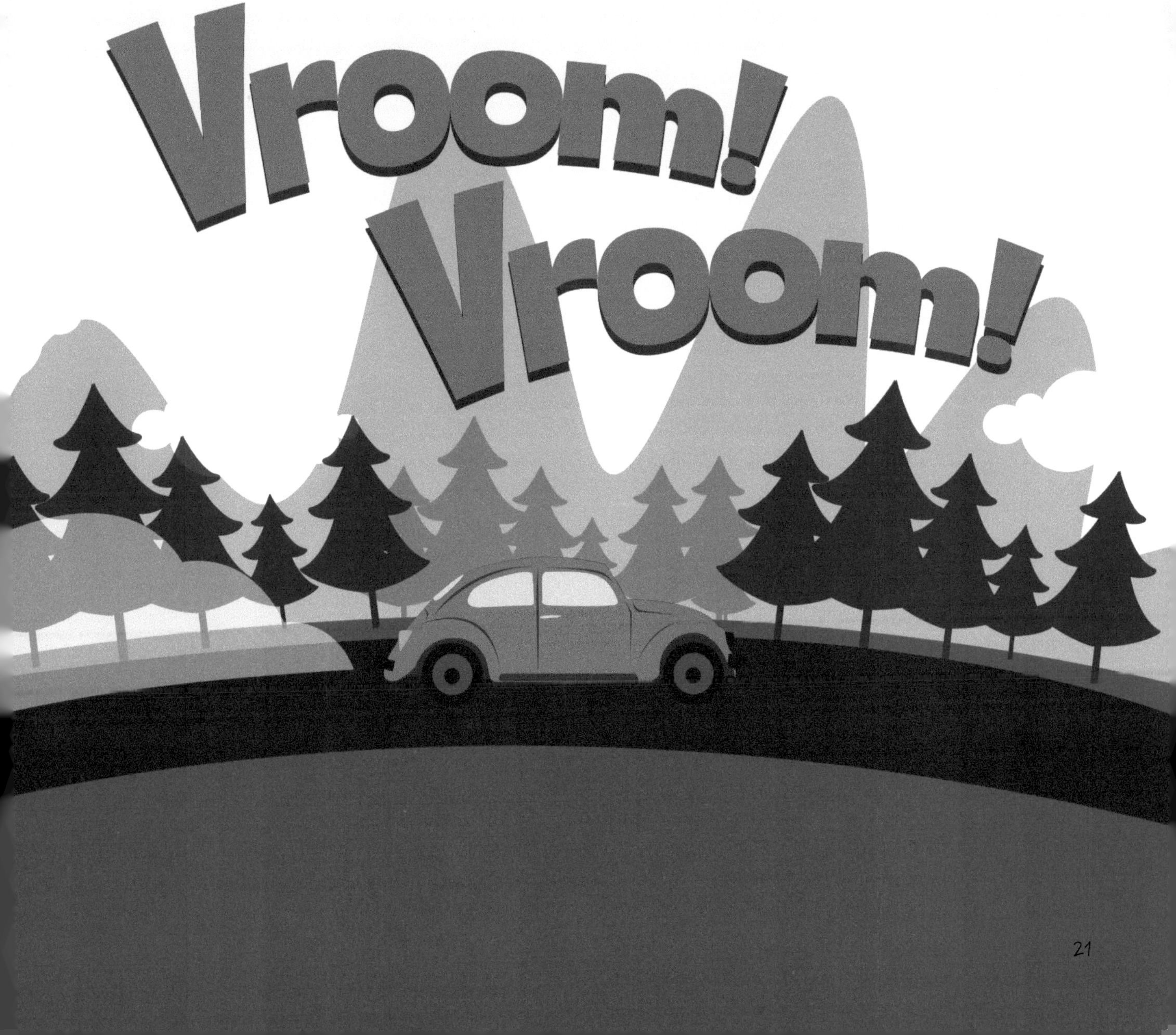
Vroom! Vroom!

Then all of a sudden, Alexander saw a road sign that warned him to slow down and to pay close attention. Sometimes during an adventure with Jesus, there will be signs from the Holy Spirit to alert us of something very important that we need to know for the journey.

23

Next, Alexander noticed some construction workers working on the road ahead. "Uh oh! We have to slow down!" Alexander shrieked. Alexander saw some construction vehicles and machines working on the job site. He saw a dump truck, a concrete mixer truck, a bulldozer, a front-end loader, and an excavator. These machines and trucks were going to be used to install a roundabout that would help with the flow of traffic.

Once the car came to a stop, a construction worker knocked on the driver's window. He told Alexander and Jesus that they were going to have to find alternative route, because the road was out of commission for a while.

Jesus immediately pulled out His map, the Bible. Jesus's Father in Heaven had given the map to Jesus, and Jesus used the map to help Him whenever He felt confused or worried about what to do next. Jesus told Alexander that God had made all of us with a purpose, and He had a route that He wanted us to take.

"We will know we are on the right path and are going the way God wants us to go if we follow the map correctly. Even when it looks or feels like we are having to take a detour, don't worry, because God always knows the right way," Jesus said.

"So which way are you going today, Alexander? There are two paths that you can choose from. Will you choose the path that leads to destruction or the path that leads to life? It is totally up to you!" Jesus said.

"I will choose the one that leads to life!"
Alexander shouted.

"Awesome! I am so happy to hear that.
Then let's roll!" Jesus said.

35

Like Alexander, we all have a choice to decide which road we will go down. Alexander chose life. He has also chosen to use the map of God's Word (The Bible) and his friend, Jesus (His GPS), to help him get where he needs to go. Now it's up to you to decide for yourself.

Will you choose life?

Memory Verses:

Proverbs 3: 1-8

My son, do not forget my law, but let your heart keep my commands;
For length of days and long life and peace they will add to you.

Let not mercy and truth forsake you;
Bind them around your neck,
Write them on the tablet of your heart,
And so find favor and high esteem
In the sight of God and man.

Trust in the Lord with all your heart,
And lean not on your own understanding;
In all your ways acknowledge Him,
And he shall direct your paths.

Do not be wise in your own eyes;
Fear the Lord and depart from evil.
It will be health to your flesh,
and strength to your bones.

About the Author

Ashton is a wife and mother of two children. Before she changed professions to become a stay-at-home mom, Ashton worked in the public school as a middle school counselor. She has also spent time working as a teacher at the preschool level. She holds a master's degree in education, as well as a bachelor's degree in psychology. Her leading goal in life is to raise godly children and to teach them to go into the world to make a difference in the lives of others. She also desires to bring young children into God's family by teaching them the truth of God's Word.

CPSIA information can be obtained
at www.ICGtesting.com
Printed in the USA
BVHW021616220222
629769BV00002B/27